Diamond Hunt

Hazel Townson

Andersen Press • London

First published in 2003 by
Andersen Press Limited,
20 Vauxhall Bridge Road, London SW1V 2SA
www.andersenpress.co.uk

Reprinted in 2006, 2007

British Library Cataloguing in Publication Data available
ISBN 978 1 84270 302 1

Phototypeset by Intype Libra Ltd
Printed in the UK by CPI Bookmarque, Croydon, CR0 4TD

For my daughter Catherine, with love
and thanks

LIST OF MAIN CHARACTERS

ADAM SYKES – a temporary pupil at St Hilda's school

LUCY MELLING – a permanent pupil at St Hilda's school

ROB AND MYRA MELLING – Lucy's aunt and uncle with whom Lucy is staying whilst her mother is in hospital

VINCENT SHARKEY – a local villain

CYNTHIA BLAKE – partner-in-crime to Vincent Sharkey

FIONA BLAKE – mother of Cynthia

GLORIA WILSON – Myra Melling's next-door neighbour and old school friend of Fiona Blake

PROLOGUE

The most intriguing tales of real-life
happenings often come to us bit by
bit. We gather little scraps of
information here and there, which we
have to fit together with other scraps
until the whole picture is finally
revealed. This is just such a tale,
coming gradually to light from many
sources. It is the tale of a valuable
diamond. Many years ago this
diamond was bought by a rich banker
to be made into a brooch for his
daughter's coming of age. But the
daughter was suddenly and tragically
killed in a riding accident, and the
diamond was put away in a secret
drawer at the back of a dressing-table
where it remained undiscovered after
its owner died. The dressing-table

1

changed hands several times by way of various auctions and good-as-new stores but maybe the diamond is just about to be re-discovered . . .

PART 1
SETTLING IN

Adam Sykes on his mobile phone, Sunday, 3rd

– *Hi, Dad! See? I got here OK, but I don't know why they call this place Bonnydale, it's anything but.*

 – No, no problems. The bus driver remembered to yell out when it was my stop and Gran was waiting there to meet me. She was a bit fed up because the bus was half an hour late and her knees were playing her up, but she says it'll be useful having me around. I can help out with the shopping and launderette (groan, groan!).

 – Yeah, I AM being good. I even made up my own bed as Gran reckons she finds it hard climbing the stairs now. She says once a day is enough. You could write rude words in the dust on

my ancient dressing-table and there are big balls of grey fluff under the bed. Still, I found some fairly clean sheets and pillowcases and a duvet cover with racing cars on that she once won at Bingo, so it's not so bad.

– Yes, Dad, I HAVE given my mind to it, but you know what I said about this St Hilda's school? Well, I was right. I've just been round there to suss it out and it's stuck among a load of posh houses right at the other end of the village. Bound to be the toffee-nosed sort where all the kids can read before they start in Infants and all the mums go begging the teachers to set extra homework. Picture me in a dump like that!

– I WILL try to settle in. I promised, didn't I? But I'm gonna miss Dave and Simon something rotten. So don't leave me here too long, will you, Dad?

*It feels like the back of beyond,
especially with Gran not having a
computer or even a video, and only one
telly. A good thing you bought me this
mobile or I think I'd have gone barmy.*

*– No, I WON'T bankrupt you with
it. I'll only ring a couple of times a
week and maybe another couple of
times to Dave and Simon.*

*– All right then, just you and Dave
at weekends.*

*– Yeah, I know you're busy, but once
you've got the inquest and funeral over
with I could come home right away. I
could even come back in time for the
funeral. I wouldn't be in the way or
make a big fuss. In fact I could look
after you. Gran reckons I make a good
skivvy and I'm learning to cook after
a fashion. I had to make our dinner as
soon as I got here. Besides, I reckon
Jenny would have wanted me to be at*

7

*her funeral, if only to show we were
parting on good terms.*

*– Yes, she would! I know she was
only my step-mum but we got on OK
most of the time.*

*– Well, I don't mind feeling miserable
for a bit, honest. Everybody feels
miserable at funerals anyway, and I
don't care if the police start asking me
more questions. They were OK last
time.*

*– Oh, all right if you say so. But if I
stop here I'm gonna need something
to fill the time in. You could send my
Game Boy on for a start. I forgot it in
the rush. Some more funds wouldn't go
amiss, either.*

*– Cheers, Dad, and don't you be
down in the dumps. You and me'll
have some great times when all this is
over, just the two of us. So keep your
spirits up.*

Letter from Lucy Melling to her mother, Monday, 4th

Aunty Myra's,
Bonnydale.
Monday 4th

Dear Mum,

I hope you have settled in to hospital OK. Aunty Myra says I can't come to see you for a while but I can write to you whenever I like and she will make sure you get the letters.

I'm doing fine here so you needn't worry about me. Aunty Myra's a good cook and she's given me the biggest back bedroom with frilly pink curtains and two wardrobes (one of them deep enough to hide in!). There's even a swinging mirror on the dressing-table.

Uncle Rob says it's lucky he works nights so he can take me to school in his car before he goes to bed in the mornings and collect me first thing when he gets up in the afternoons. I told him he didn't need to, I could easily walk, but he says it's twice as far from here to St Hilda's as it was from our house. So what? I could still do it in fifteen minutes tops. Anyway, if it makes him feel useful I daresay I'll let him drive me, especially if it's raining.

Today a new boy turned up all the way from Carfield. He's called Adam Sykes, he's in our class and Miss Garner asked me to look after him. I showed him where everything was and lent him a ruler and even sat with him at dinner time but he didn't say much or even smile. Everyone reckons he's sulky but I think he's just feeling out of it. It's rotten not knowing anybody and having to leave all your friends behind. I'm glad I didn't have to leave St Hilda's and split from Kay and Tracy.

We had shepherd's pie for supper and cherry tart for afters. They let me have ice cream on mine instead of custard, you know how I hate that stuff. I hope your hospital food is good, but don't worry if it isn't: Aunty M is going to bring you some fruit and cake. I told her you didn't like green grapes, only black ones with no pips.

After you'd gone to hospital I had a look round your bedroom for something I could keep with me to remind me of you, I hope you don't mind. At first I thought of taking a scarf or something, but then, at the back of one of those little drawers in your dressing-table – the one that always sticks – I found this big glass bead. I expect it was part of a broken necklace that got left behind and forgotten.

I chose the bead because it's a small thing, easy to hide so I can keep it more private. I've made a little cloth bag for it and hung it on a ribbon round my neck and nobody knows I've got it, not even Aunty M. I even wear it in bed. It's our secret and it really is the next best thing to having a bit of you still here. I think of you every time I see or feel it.

I'll write again soon if we don't get a lot of homework but it takes me a long time to do a whole letter. I'm not a fast writer and I have to keep looking up the spellings. Uncle Rob says he'll try to think of a better solution, but I don't know what he has in mind.

Lots of love,
Lucy

P.S. I might get picked for the school choir, I'll let you know.

**E-mail message sent to Cynthia
Blake by Vincent Sharkey of
Albert Buildings, Stebbings,
Monday, 4th**

*Cyn, you ring me as soon as you get
in. I think we've hit the jackpot.
Remember me going on about this
article I saw in a magazine at the
dentist's, about this rich Victorian
bloke who used to live round here?
He bought a whacking great diamond
for his daughter, then she got killed
so he hid it away. That diamond's
actually famous and it's worth a
bloomin' fortune. Well, I went down
the library and looked up some old
newspaper articles about him; found
out where he used to live and stuff
like that. It turns out he was the last*

14

one of his family, so his home got
sold up after he died and the money
raised went to charity. Most of the
furniture was auctioned, and get this
– he's supposed to have hidden that
diamond in his dressing-table,
although nobody could ever find it.
So I did some more snooping and I
reckon I've even tracked down the
dressing-table. It's been through four
owners but I doubt it'll move again
for a while. What's the betting it's got
a secret drawer somewhere?

Right now it's in a house just
outside a village called Bonnydale.
I'm going over there to have a look at
it tonight and I want you to come
with me for back-up – know what I
mean? Meet me outside Stebbings
chapel at ten o'clock. Wear something
dark and bring an extra pair of tights.

And don't be late. We'll have a fair old drive, and I've no time to mess about.

16

Adam Sykes on his mobile phone, Monday, 4th

– Hi, Dad, it's me again.

– Yeah, I'm OK. Can't grumble, though Gran's meals aren't up to much, especially when I have to cook 'em. I'm losing more weight than a champion jockey.

– Tell you what, I was right about St Hilda's, they all think they're the bees' knees, especially the girls. There's one called Lucy Melling who reckons she's going to mother me, but she's in for a shock. Picture me being mothered!

– 'Course I'm helping out. Got no choice, have I? I even took Gran's bedding to the launderette after school. She must have been saving it up for ages; I could hardly carry it. Then I

17

had to peel the spuds and fry the fish fingers. Gran doesn't even have a microwave, would you believe? I'm getting pretty fed up with being a slave, but I suppose it's good training and it means I'll be able to look after you a treat when I come back home. Better than Jenny ever did.

– No, the teachers aren't so bad, except for this Miss Garner who kept me back after school for a bit of nosy-parkering. She asked about you and Jenny so I told her Jenny wasn't around any more and she thought I meant you two had split up.

– Well, she can think what she likes, it's nobody else's business but ours.

– Oh, she's a bit of a pest altogether, that Garner. Wants me to audition for the school choir but I told her I had weak vocal cords and had to be careful not to strain my voice.

18

– Well, I could have weak vocal cords for all you know. Gran says I talk too much and I'll wear my voice out if I'm not careful.

– I don't think I'll make any friends here, all the lads are already ganged up and they're not my sort anyway, but it won't matter because I'll not be here long, will I? You'll be needing me back home.

– Oh, Dad, it's all right you saying nothing's decided yet, but I want to come back now and be with you. I miss you. I can't stop thinking about Jenny and seeing her lying there. Do you think if I'd run a bit faster to fetch you she might not have died?

– Honest? You're not just saying that?

– Well, it's not the sort of thing you can forget in a hurry. Every time I shut my eyes I get the same horrible picture.

I told the policewoman that when she questioned me but she said I should try not to think about it, it was probably just an unlucky accident.

– Yeah well, that's easier said than done. If I don't think about that, then I need something else to think about, which reminds me, don't forget to send my Game Boy, will you? I did ask you on Sunday.

– Well, you might have more important things to think about, but that's important to ME. Oh, and I need some more money, a fiver for a school outing. We're going on a coach trip to some stately home, dead exciting, I don't think!

– Cheers, Dad. Speak to you again soon. And just think about what I said. Please?

Tape recording from Lucy Melling to her mum, Tuesday, 5th

Hey, Mum, isn't this great? Uncle Rob's bought me this tape recorder so I can talk to you properly and not have to spend so much time writing letters. Aunty M's going to bring it with her when she comes to see you, and this is the best bit, if ever you feel like talking back to me you'll be able to.

Aunty M tells us you were feeling a bit better yesterday, though that doesn't mean you'll be home soon. She says the mind doesn't heal as fast as the body and the bump on your head made you lose your memory for a bit. But I'm sure you'll get it back soon. When can I come and see you? I won't mind if you can't be bothered doing your hair or getting dressed and stuff, or if you don't want to talk. I could just sit and hold your hand for a bit.

Shall I tell you all the school news next? Guess what, I got a gold star for my maths project! Uncle Rob says at this rate I'll be able to work out his income tax for him next year. I did an audition for the choir as well, but I won't know until next week whether I'm in it or not. Cross fingers for me, I love a good singalong.

Oh, and I asked if I could invite this new boy Adam Sykes back for tea on Saturday. Aunty M said she didn't see why not. But you know what, all he said when I asked him was, 'What for?' So I told him, 'You and I have got something in common, or haven't you noticed? We're both in the same boat, missing our folks and having to live with different people for a while so maybe we should stick together.'

He gave me a funny look and said maybe he'd think about it. I even told him Uncle Rob would come for him in the car if he wanted, but he said did I think he hadn't any legs, or what. Talk about rude! I don't know why I bother, except that I feel sorry for him. Mr and Mrs Wilson next door to Aunty M have got relatives in Carfield, where Adam comes from, and they told us Adam's step-mum just died in an accident, that's why he's here. It was in all the papers over there. She fell down the stairs and broke her neck, isn't that awful?

Aunty M's taking me to the pictures tomorrow night. She says I'm good company while Uncle Rob's on nights, otherwise she wouldn't get out much.

I wish you were coming with us, but never mind, I've still got our little secret contact, remember? Your bead round my neck. So a bit of you will be there with us. Take care, Mum. I love you lots.

E-mail from Mrs Gloria Wilson, Bonnydale, to her sister Mrs Fiona Blake, Carfield, Tuesday, 5th

Hi, Fee! I'm getting the hang of this computer now. Great, isn't it? Who said us old fogies couldn't join the technical revolution?

I've posted you that jumper pattern you wanted. It turned out a bit too long when I did it, so miss a few rows out of the middle.

Life here's not very exciting just now. I hope it's better with you. The only thing that's happened all week is that Rob and Myra next door have had their niece Lucy dumped on them all of a sudden. Poor little thing, her mum's in Langways Psychiatric Hospital and from what I can gather she'll be there for a few weeks yet. Apparently she got bashed on the head when she was mugged on her way back from the market, so she's got some sort of brain damage, lost her memory or something. The muggers took her handbag but there was only three pounds fifty in it plus a bit of make-up and her front door key. Honestly, the things that happen these days! It makes you terrified to go anywhere.

Young Lucy thinks her mum's illness will all clear up in a day or two, like chicken-pox, and I just hope she's right. Rob's bought the kid a tape recorder so that she can send her mum messages, but what they're really hoping is that the sound of the kid's voice will do the mum some good and bring her memory back. Well, you never know.

I can't help thinking it's hard luck on Rob and Myra, being stuck with that child for goodness knows how long when they've got set in their ways and never wanted kids of their own. I don't suppose they know much about bringing up kids. Rob has to drive her to school every morning when he's just come off the night shift, then he's got to pick her up again at half past three before he's properly finished his sleep. He won't keep that up for long, you mark my words! I'd let her walk if it was me. Kids get spoiled to death these days. It never did us any harm to walk to school, did it? (Remember those two lads from the Comp who used to follow us? Kept shouting after us, calling us the Terrible Twins? Those were the days, eh?)

Love to Harry. Mail us back when you've time.

E-mail from Mrs Fiona Blake to her sister Mrs Gloria Wilson, Tuesday, 5th

Who are you calling an old fogy?? Speak for yourself – I'm a wiz on this computer. I can even do fancy borders and shadow lettering.

Ta for the pattern. I got it this morning, only I can't get started yet because the shop's run out of lavender wool.

Yeah, I remember those lads from the Comp. That one called Russell really fancied you. He has a butcher's shop in Swindon now, see what you missed?

I think I can beat you for news. You know those neighbours of ours I told you about? That Jenny Sykes who broke her neck falling down the stairs? Well, we had a rare bit of excitement today. Two detectives were round at ours asking questions. Harry says that's because they've suddenly decided she didn't fall, she was pushed! At first when it happened the police talked to the boy who was there when she fell, and they decided it was just an accident. But now it's come out that this Jenny and her husband had a bust-up earlier that night. Some of the neighbours have said they could hear them going at it hammer and tongs. There's been police swarming all over the place, just like a telly thriller. There's an inquest soon, so I'll let you know what happens. After they'd questioned the boy – Adam, he's called – his dad bundled him off to his gran's in Bonnydale, so maybe you'll come across him.

Our Cynthia still hasn't rung. Last I heard, she was living in Stebbings, in a flat over a cake shop. Fat lot of good that'll do her figure! She's got no proper job yet as far as I know but she never seems to be short of money. I can't help worrying about her, though. Harry reckons I'm wasting my time. He says she can look after herself, no problem, because she takes after him. (That's what worries me.)

Well, I'm sorry to hear about the kid next door. I hope she won't turn out to be too much trouble.

Gotta go now, Harry's back, roaring for his supper. Keep in touch.

Telephone call to Cynthia Blake from Vincent Sharkey, Tuesday, 5th

– Cyn, it's me. Where the dickens were you? I waited over half an hour last night then had to press on without you.

– Well, that's no excuse. And if that's the way you're going to carry on, then you needn't expect any share of the profits this time.

– You don't deserve to know what happened.

– Well, what do you think? Would I be bothering to ring you up if I'd found the bloomin' diamond?

– Of course I got there, no problem, and no, there wasn't anybody at home. I sneaked in OK as well, no

thanks to you, but I got no joy after that. Spent half the blessed night in there. Sussed out all the likely hiding places, trapped my fingers, banged my shins, fell over twice and ripped my jacket getting through the window, but nothing doing. Came up with plenty of other rubbish, but no signs of what I really wanted.

– Yes, well, I was pretty sick too, I can tell you, after all that planning. Waste of a good, moonless night, as well. Then just to add insult to injury I thought I'd been spotted on the way out so I had to make a long detour and ran out of petrol half a mile from home. That's what happens when you've got no lookout. Don't you dare let me down again.

– Yes, well, this'll be your last chance, and don't you forget it!

– All right then, if you swear you

won't let me down again, here's what
you can do. It turns out the old girl
who lives there has been whisked off
to hospital so maybe she's taken her
little nest-egg with her. So what I
want you to do now is to find out
which hospital she's in and go and
visit her.

– 'Course you can! Pretend to be a
long-lost relative, or somebody from
the Social.

– Oh, for goodness' sake use your
imagination for once, can't you? She
won't know who you are, she'll be
seeing strangers all the time. Take her
some flowers and chat her up a bit.
Find out all you can, and have a good
root through her locker while you're
there. And this time just DO IT or
you're dumped.

PART 2
A KIND OF FRIENDSHIP

Lucy Melling's tape recording to her mum, Sunday, 10th

Hi, Mum, it's me again, signing in for another chat. How are you doing?

I told you about asking that boy Adam Sykes to come for tea on Saturday, didn't I? Well, he never turned up. Aunty Myra got the best cloth out as well, and she let me help her bake a special cake. I put the icing on the top all by myself, white with pink and purple squiggles, you should have seen it.

First I was disappointed, then I got mad. I thought at least he could have let us know he wasn't coming because I'd checked with him on Friday and he'd said OK, he'd be there. I felt a right idiot and it wasn't fair on Aunty

M. Anyway after a bit I went round to Adam's gran's to give him a piece of my mind. I couldn't get an answer at the front door so I went round the back and found him sitting on a crate in the back yard, gassing away on his mobile phone. He said I'd no business to come chasing after him, his gran's back yard was private, and it was a free country anyway so he could do what he liked. I said a promise was a promise, but he said he'd only promised to come because I kept nagging at him and he wanted to shut me up. So then I got even madder and told him he was utterly selfish and it was no wonder nobody but me would have anything to do with him. I told him he was so busy being stuck up that he'd never have any friends, just when he needed them.

Well, I thought he was going to

explode! He said he'd got plenty of friends at home, better than any of the toffee-nosed lot round here, so he didn't need any more, and anyway right now he preferred his own company.

So I said, right, that saves me a lot of trouble. Catch me and my aunty wasting any more time baking cakes, pies, sausage rolls, scones and biscuits for ungrateful yobs! I flounced off and started walking away, but then all of a sudden he changed his mind. He gave a massive great sigh and said all right, if the food was going to waste he'd come, anything for a bit of peace, he didn't know what all the fuss was about. I said, 'Please yourself, I'm past caring,' and walked off, but he followed me.

So we went back for our tea after all, but not before he'd slammed his gran's gate and broken a piece off it. Temper, temper! He'll be in trouble when she sees it, and serve him right. Anyway, we made up and I must say he ate a good tea, including four pies, all the scones and most of the cake and biscuits. You'd have thought he hadn't eaten for a month! Still, we managed to save a slice of cake for you. Aunty M's bringing it with this message. Let me know if you like it.

I hope you are OK, Mum, and not too sad. I think about you all the time. I've still got your bead round my neck. It feels really good and I'm sure it brings me luck. Adam spotted the ribbon and asked what I had round my neck, but I told him it was just my door key. It's our secret.

Lots and lots of love, Lucy

Telephone call received by Fiona Blake from her daughter, Cynthia Blake, Sunday, 10th

– Is that you, our Cynthia? Blimey, wonders never cease! Don't say you've actually bothered to ring us at last.

– Yes, well, I have tried to ring you but you're never in and I hate that bloomin' answerphone. I never know what to say to it and I'm always scared it'll answer me back in a tinny voice like some daft Dalek.

– Never mind, you're here now and it's lovely to talk to you. Everything OK, love?

– Well, I'm entitled to worry about you. I am your mother and I can't help wondering what's going on when you're miles away in a dump like Stebbings and you've got no job.

– Oh, you have got a job, have you?

41

What sort of job? Nothing illegal, I hope?

– Private investigator? What sort of a job's that supposed to be? Sounds a bit rum to me. Don't you need some sort of qualifications for that? Not that you've got any. I don't think one GCSE in woodwork will get you very far.

– Oh well, if it includes visiting hospitals I guess it can't be all that dodgy. I suppose it's better than nothing. What's the pay like?

– Payment by results? I wouldn't put up with that if I were you. You want a decent minimum wage, plus bonuses for good work. Can't you join a union? Talk to your dad about it, he knows all about stuff like that.

– I don't care how much job satisfaction you get, it's never as good as money in the bank. Anyway, you just be careful or you could finish up in all sorts of trouble. People get very stroppy if they think they're being spied on.

– Your Aunty Gloria? Fancy you

asking about her after all this time. I didn't know you cared.

– Yes, she's OK, sends you her love whenever I talk to her. We e-mail each other all the time as a matter of fact. We're not half as old-hat as you think we are. She's always saying you're to look her up next time you're anywhere near Bonnydale because she's nearly forgotten what you look like.

– Well, go and see her, then, you don't have to wait for a proper invitation. She'll be really chuffed, and she's usually in, except when she's gossiping with Rob and Myra next door. She does a lot of that lately, because those two have got their niece Lucy staying with them while her mum's in hospital. Gloria feels sorry for that kid. She even plays draughts with her.

– Well, Lucy's mum's in Langways Psychiatric Hospital and not expected to come out for a few weeks yet. Got mugged and bashed on the head.

– What do you want to know the kid's

43

surname for? She's nothing to do with you.

– Well, it's Melling as a matter of fact, but she's nobody you know. You've never even met Rob and Myra. If you ask me, this private investigator lark's already gone to your head.

– Well you shouldn't have to be 'just making conversation' with your own mother.

– Oh, go on with you! Ring me again next week, then, and tell me how your new job's going. I think we deserve a bit of news now and then, don't you?

– No, I'm not a fusspot, I just care about you, and don't you forget it! Your dad will be sorry he's missed you, he's down the pub as usual, but he'd have sent his love as well as me if he'd been in.

OK, 'bye then, and don't forget what I said – keep in touch.

E-mail from Cynthia Blake to Vincent Sharkey, Monday, 11th

– Now, Vin, just drop everything and listen to this, then take back all you said about me never keeping in touch or doing my bit. Talk about speed and efficiency! I've already tracked down the hospital that Melling woman's in and I actually went there this afternoon. Mind you, I soon found out it would be a waste of time trying to talk to her, it's one of these psychiatric places and she's completely off her trolley for a while. Seems she was mugged and got a nasty knock on the head. (I don't think that mugger got away with what we're looking for, though, because it says in the paper she only had three pounds fifty on her, plus a few groceries.)

Anyway, crafty me, I found out from one of the nurses that her sister-in-law Myra visits her most afternoons, so I hung around in the waiting-room until this Myra turned up. Then I sat next to her and got talking. We had a lovely long chat. It turns out she's not only the patient's sister-in-law but she's actually looking after the Melling kid AND she lives right next door to my Aunt Gloria. Would you believe it? Talk about hitting the jackpot!

'Course, I had to pretend I was visiting somebody else at the hospital. I made up a whole case-history for my non-existent potty granddad, then said I'd come all that way for nothing, as they'd just discharged him! (Honestly, I ought to be writing best-sellers or telly scripts.) I hung around until this Myra came out again, and I could see she was a bit upset so I took her for a cup of tea. After that, surprise, surprise! She couldn't help confiding in caring old me. She says this visiting is all stressful stuff and the worst bit is reporting back to the kid who is really missing her mum and expecting her home any minute.

Now get this – the kid wears a keepsake of her mum's tucked up in a little cloth bag on a ribbon round her neck! Some sort of bead, Myra reckons, or maybe a lucky charm. It's supposed to be a secret so they all pretend they don't know about it but the kid let it slip on this tape recorder she has for sending messages to her mum. If that bead's not what we're looking for I'll paint my nails with creosote.

So go on then, congratulate me, and

don't just call it luck. It was a stroke of genius on my part, plus good connections and even better management. The name Bonnydale struck a chord because of me having an aunt over there, and since little Lucy's good old Aunty Myra actually lives right next door to my aunt, I'm going to pay the pair of them a nice, friendly visit, moving in fast before anybody has a chance to guess what we're up to.

Won't our Myra be pleased to see me again, kind, sympathetic soul that I am? Even more so when I turn even kinder by being specially sweet to the kid. I aim to offer my services in helping to look after young Lucy, meeting her out of school, for instance, or taking her off her aunty's hands for a while by arranging a picnic to some

nice, lonely spot. Plenty of
possibilities, eh?

Well then, am I worth my weight in
diamonds, or what? I'll keep in touch
and give you regular progress reports
but if you want to talk to me about
any of this you'll either have to ring
back pretty sharpish or get me on the
mobile. Or you can e-mail me, as I'll
be taking the laptop. I'm leaving for
Bonnydale in just over an hour.

Lucy Melling's tape recording, Tuesday, 12th

It's me again, Mum. Hope you're getting on all right. Aunty M said you listened to all my last tape and she thought it made you smile, though you weren't well enough to talk back to me.

The Wilsons next door have got a visitor called Cynthia who's come to stay for a bit. She's Mrs Wilson's niece, and guess what, she called in tonight and brought me a coral necklace for a present. She knew about you being in hospital and said I was a very brave girl. She wanted to fasten the necklace on for me but it was bedtime so Aunty M said we'd better leave it until tomorrow. Don't worry, though,

I won't swap it for your bead, I'll just wear both at once if I have to. I can't wear a proper necklace to school anyway, it's against the rules.

I got picked for the choir, and so did Tracy and Adam. Adam said he didn't want to be in it, but Miss Garner said he had to because they were short of boys. We'll have to practise every Tuesday and Thursday, starting this week, so that we'll be ready to sing at the school Open Day. Once we've got that over I'm going to ask Miss Garner if she can arrange for the choir to come to your hospital to sing for the patients. (That's if you aren't already home by then.) We could put a special programme together and cheer you all up. Wouldn't that be great, Mum?

We're going on a school outing tomorrow to a place called Addenby

Hall so I expect I'll have lots to tell you next time.

Keep your chin up, Mum, it won't be long before you're better. Love you!

E-mail from Gloria Wilson to Fiona Blake, Wednesday, 13th

Well, wonders never cease; your Cynthia has turned up at long last! I nearly put the red carpet out for this great occasion as we thought she'd written us off altogether. I must say she's quite a looker now she's lost some of her puppy fat, and she's a lot more thoughtful than she used to be. She turned up with a big bouquet of roses for me, a six-pack for Jim and a present for that poor child next door. Apparently she'd bumped into Myra somewhere and heard all about their troubles. We're all dead impressed as your Cyn has even offered to meet young Lucy out of school every day to save Rob having to get up early when he's on nights. Rob says he'll certainly be grateful for a bit of help on two nights a week at any rate, because

young Lucy's having choir practice
Tuesdays and Thursdays so she won't
be finished until after Rob's gone to
work. I never had your lass down for
a do-gooder – can a leopard change its
spots? But don't get me wrong, we're
not complaining.

I don't suppose you know how long
she's intending to stay, do you? (Not
that she isn't welcome, it's lovely to see
her.) I did ask her but she was a bit
vague. She said it all depends on her
job, but I didn't even know she had
one. See if you can find out when she
rings you.

How's your jumper coming on? It's a
complicated pattern so don't try to
knit while you're watching telly. I got
into a right mess that way. Had to pull
half of it back.

Fancy that Russell turning out to be
a butcher! I had him down for an
astronaut at the very least, the way he
used to go on about space travel.
Anyway, it's a good job I didn't fall for

him, I've been a vegetarian since that BSE scare.

Let me know about your Cynthia's plans as soon as possible.

E-mail from Fiona Blake to Gloria Wilson, Wednesday, 13th

Our Cyn is on a special job, that's why she doesn't know how long she'll be stopping with you. It's all a bit hush-hush because get this – she's working as a private investigator and she'll have to stick around until everything's sorted out. The case she's on is something to do with a hospital over in your neck of the woods, but don't let on that I told you. I bet some newborn baby's been kidnapped from Maternity or some doctor's made a daft mistake, like chopping the wrong leg off or something. Or you never know, she might even be after that Melling woman's mugger; they haven't caught anybody yet. Anyway, she's looking for clues and she'll have to see it through, even if it takes weeks. You don't mind, do you? I'd rather she stayed with you than in some sleazy digs. She could pay you some board now she's working, so don't you be out of pocket.

Harry's that proud of her, you'd think she'd just been made Prime Minister, but I'm not so sure she's on to a good thing. It sounds a bit risky to me. See what you can find out about it, will you, especially if there's any guns involved? Do a bit of spying yourself, and get her talking. She'll probably tell you more than she tells me, I'm only her mother.

I'd be a vegetarian myself if it wasn't for Harry. He won't do without his bloomin' chops and beefburgers and a roast on a Sunday, and he gets through more bacon than a Tesco slicer.

Lucy Melling's tape recording, Wednesday, 13th

Hello again, Mum! It was the big day today when we went on this trip to Addenby Hall. I wish you could have seen it. Miss Garner says it's Elizabethan, a great big house built like a big letter E, in lots of gardens with statues all over the place. Lord Addenby still lives there some of the time but he wasn't in today. Instead there was a nice lady with grey hair who said she was in the Guides, though she didn't have a uniform. She showed us round everywhere and told us all about the furniture and the pictures. I had a great time, I thought it was all really interesting. They had four-poster beds and warming pans

and the children used to have to do
embroidery all the time and then have
it framed. There was a big spit in the
kitchen to put a whole pig on, and
there was even a dungeon. You can't
please everybody, though. Some of our
class got bored, especially Adam
Sykes who kept wandering away on
his own. He was supposed to be my
partner for the day, so I had to keep
sneaking off to fetch him back in case
he got lost and missed the coach home.

One time when I went after him he
was standing at the top of this great
big staircase staring down at the steps
like somebody in a trance and he
didn't half jump when I went up to
him. It's a wonder he didn't go
crashing to the bottom. I asked him if
he was daydreaming or what, and he
told me to mind my own business.
Then he ran off down the stairs and I

would have run after him if I hadn't
heard Miss Garner shouting to us to
come back. But who do you think I
spotted coming up the stairs just
then? It was that nice lady called
Cynthia, the one I told you about who
is visiting the Wilsons next door. I was
really surprised to see her. She said
she'd heard about the school trip from
Aunty M and thought she'd come
along too as it sounded like a nice day
out. She wanted to take me for an ice
cream but I said I had to stick with the
others or I'd be in trouble. Then Miss
Garner turned up looking flustered
and said I shouldn't be talking to
strangers. I said Cynthia wasn't a
stranger so I introduced her, and
Cynthia gave her a great big smile
and offered to help. Miss Garner
looked relieved, I think she was
finding us all a bit of a handful, so she

said Cynthia could go and fetch Adam back if she wouldn't mind, and she sent me with her so I could point him out.

I knew Adam had turned right at the bottom of the stairs but Cynthia reckoned we should turn left and head him off. We didn't come across him, though. We finished up in a bushy part of the garden where there was nobody about. Cynthia said she was out of breath and we'd better sit down for a minute, so we sat on a wall. Then she asked if I was wearing the necklace she'd given me and I said no, I wasn't allowed. She said are you sure? What's that I can see round your neck? But just then Miss Garner and the others turned up. They'd found Adam already and he'd been told to stay right by the teacher for the rest of the day. I think Cynthia was disappointed because I wasn't wearing her necklace. She looked a bit miffed, then suddenly remembered she had something else to do and went off in a hurry. So then Miss Garner was miffed as well, though Cynthia had tried her best. Some people are never satisfied!

I'll have to go now, Mum. Aunty M says it's bedtime but I'll talk to you again soon. Sleep tight! Lots of love.

Adam Sykes on his mobile to his friend David, Wednesday, 13th

– *Wotcher, Dave, how's tricks?*

– *What do YOU think? How would you like to live with your gran, no computer, no video, no nothing? It's like going back to the Middle Ages. It had better not be for long, I can tell you!*

– *Don't talk to me about school! I hate this toffee-nosed St Hilda's lot. I don't know who's worse, the kids or the teachers. Can you believe it, they've even put me in the rotten choir? Me, with a voice like a turkey! And there's this girl called Lucy Melling who keeps hanging round me all the time. She invited me to tea last weekend and I had to go because I was starving.*

– No, honest! Gran's meals are the pits, never enough to feed a mouse and hardly worth eating anyway.

– Well, food's important, I happen to be a growing lad.

– 'Course I don't fancy her! She's only a kid.

– Well, I can feel sorry for her, can't I? She's got no dad and her mum's in a loony bin. Besides, nobody else bothers to talk to me. Like I said, they're a right stuck-up lot. We even had to trail round this Lord Muck's stately home today and gawp at all his mouldy old furniture. What a bore!

– Anyway, listen, I've been trying to ring my dad for ages but I can't get hold of him. Do you know where he is?

– You WHAT? Taken in for questioning? You must be joking!

– *You mean, the police think he had something to do with Jenny's death?*

– *But he couldn't have! I already explained to them . . .*

– *No, I happen to know he couldn't have because I was there. I had to run and fetch him, and he was halfway to the pub when she fell.*

– *So? I don't care what the rotten cops say, they've got it wrong. I already told them it was an accident and they should have talked to me again first. I'll just have to come over there and put them straight.*

– *Yes, I can. I got myself here and I'll get myself back again, it's not that difficult.*

– *Keep out of it? How can I keep out of it? That's my dad they've banged up, although he hasn't done anything wrong. If it were your dad you*

*wouldn't sit by and do nothing, would
you?*

*– Yeah well, you can warn me off
until you're blue in the face, but I'm
coming over as soon as I can fix it. You
just watch me!*

Conversation between Adam Sykes and Lucy Melling in the school playground at morning break, Thursday, 14th

ADAM: Hey, Lucy! Over here, I want to talk to you.

LUCY: Go on, then.

ADAM: Can you keep a secret?

LUCY: 'Course I can. What do you take me for?

ADAM: All right, get off your high horse. It's just that I'm going to tell you something really important and if it gets out I'll be in big trouble – and so will you.

LUCY: Girls do know how to keep secrets, believe it or not.

ADAM: Right then, listen. Something urgent's come up and I have to get

67

back to Carfield to see my dad but I haven't enough money for the fare. Can you lend me a couple of quid?

LUCY: I might. When are you going?

ADAM: As soon as I get the money.

LUCY: What, like tomorrow? But you can't just take off in the middle of a term.

ADAM: Who says I can't? There are more important things in life than dying of boredom in a crummy old classroom.

LUCY: Well, I hope you're going to fix it with Miss Garner first. You weren't exactly in her good books yesterday, what with all that wandering off. Still, if you've got a proper reason she won't mind, she's not a bad old stick. But disappear without telling her and you could get suspended.

ADAM: Big deal! Anyway, if you don't
want to help me . . .

LUCY: Who says I don't?

ADAM: Right then, when can I have
the money?

LUCY: Can't you borrow it from your
gran?

ADAM: No way! If she finds out I'm
going she'll just try to stop me.

LUCY: Well, I've only got fifty pence
right now, but there's a good bit
more at home in my money-box. I'll
bring it tomorrow.

ADAM: Tomorrow's too late. Can't you
fetch it at lunch time?

LUCY: No, I can't. You know very well
we're not allowed out at lunch time.
Surely one more day won't make
much difference. Why do you have
to go off in such a big hurry,
anyway?

ADAM: Never you mind. Let's just say

69

it's a matter of life and death. Can you get the money straight after school today? I could come home with you to pick it up.

LUCY: (reluctantly) All right then, but it won't be straight after school. We've got choir practice tonight, remember?

ADAM: (groaning) I'd forgotten about that. Still, it's not important; we could easily skip it for once.

LUCY: No, we can't. Miss Garner's depending on us. It's only a couple of weeks to the Open Day. She'll start a big hue-and-cry if we don't turn up, and she'll never grant you any favours after that.

ADAM: (with a massive sigh) Oh, all right then, I'll come with you after choir practice.

LUCY: By the way, I was saving that money up to buy a present for my

Aunty Myra. It's her birthday a week
on Saturday so I hope you can pay
me back before then.

ADAM: No problem. Just make sure
you get it.

LUCY: There's the bell, come on!

ADAM: After choir, then, and don't you
dare let me down.

Telephone call from Mrs Myra Melling to her next-door neighbour, Mrs Gloria Wilson, Thursday evening, 14th

– *Gloria? It's me, Myra. You haven't got our Lucy there, have you? Only she's not come home from choir practice and your Cynthia was supposed to be picking her up. I didn't ask her to, she came and offered, seeing as Rob's on nights and she knew he'd have to set off for work before the choir practice finished.*

– Well, I suppose they could have got stuck in traffic, but it's not very likely round here, especially now it's long past the rush-hour.

– Yes, I know it's early yet, but I am worried. That girl's my responsibility while her mum's in hospital. I should have gone to the school myself to

fetch her, only when your Cynthia offered I didn't want her to think I couldn't trust her.

– Yes, I've tried the school, there's only the caretaker there now and he hasn't seen her. He says the last of the choir went home ages ago.

– Well, I rang her friend Tracy – she's in the choir as well – but she didn't know anything either. Just that Lucy came out of school a bit ahead of the others, so if Cynthia had been picking her up the car could have driven off before Tracy got there.

– Do you reckon the car could have broken down? It isn't exactly an up-to-date model. As for a proper accident, I daren't even think about that.

– No, I haven't rung the hospital; do you think I should? Oh, my God, Gloria, if anything's happened to that girl I'll never forgive myself.

– How can I calm down? I just feel so helpless.

– Well, I'll give them another half an hour, then I'll have to think about ringing the police. You'll let me know right away if you hear anything, won't you?

Cynthia Blake on her mobile to Vincent Sharkey, Thursday evening, 14th

– Vin? I'm in big trouble and I need your advice quick.

– No, I haven't done anything daft, but somebody else has. I'm sitting in my car up on Stebbings moor. I went to meet the Melling kid out of school today after her choir practice, as arranged, but she had her boyfriend with her . . .

– Well, how did I know she had a boyfriend? Anyway, she said he was going home with her because he wanted to borrow something of hers, so I offered them both a lift.

– It was that or nothing, believe me.

They were obviously determined to stick together so what else could I do?

– I know I was supposed to get the girl on her own, but things don't always work out to plan, as you should know better than anybody.

'Course I realised the boy might be trouble, but I thought I'd be able to get rid of him later on.

– I don't know how; I was working on it. Oh, it's easy for you to criticise, you weren't there.

– Well, shut up and listen. When I first stopped to offer them a lift the boy gave me a really dirty look. He said they didn't take lifts from strangers, but Lucy told him I wasn't a stranger so after a bit more argument she persuaded him to get in the back seat with her. The lad still grumbled on a bit but I just ignored him.

– I know it was risky, but you're a fine one to start talking about risk, the things you make me do.

– Well, I certainly don't do them for love.

– Just LISTEN, will you? It didn't take me long to realise that I couldn't make any progress with the girl while this lad was sitting on the back seat, so I decided to drive them over to my flat. I thought I might manage to get her on her own for a minute there, just long enough to sort things out. I'd have taken them back home afterwards, whether you wanted me to or not.

– Of course they kicked up a fuss! When I shot right through the village and they realised I was heading for Stebbings the boy started yelling, calling me a kidnapper and plenty of other nasty things.

– But that wasn't all. He's a right

one, he is. He started banging on the window and carrying on. I just laughed and told him not to be silly, I was just taking them for a treat. I said I lived over a cake shop and got everything half price so we were going to have a slap-up tea.

– All right then, Lord Brainbox, what would you have said?

– The girl didn't seem too bothered actually, but the boy kept on shouting the odds and using some pretty ripe language into the bargain. Talk about urban poetry! He reckoned it was urgent for him to be somewhere else, but I guess that was just an excuse to make me stop. Then he undid his seat belt and started pulling my hair and thumping me on the shoulder. He hurt me, too; he was a vicious little beggar.

– Yes, but wait till I've finished the tale, can't you? We got nearly there and

we were just coming over the moors
ready to drop down into Stebbings
when the boy went berserk. He leaned
right over the back of my seat and
grabbed the hand-brake. I was so
startled I skidded to a stop and before
I realised what was happening he'd
leapt out of the car, dragged the girl
after him and scarpered. Last I saw of
them they were legging it across the
moors.

– No, I can't drive across that boggy
ground and I haven't a hope of
catching them on foot, me in my
stilettos. Have a bit of sense, Vin!

– So what do I do now? You're the
boss, you'd better think of something
fast or I'm heading for big trouble.
What with all this Childline stuff these
days, you can't even smile at a kid
without tangling with the law.

– Well, just you bear in mind that

we're in this together, you and me.
I've no intention of taking the rap all
by myself.

   – All right, I'll give you five minutes
to think. If you haven't rung me back
by then I'll make my own decisions
and I can promise you, you won't like
them.

Conversation between Adam Sykes and Lucy Melling on their way across Stebbings moor, Thursday evening, 14th

LUCY: Adam, stop dragging me! I don't know what you're playing at; you nearly caused an accident, leaping out of the car like that. Cynthia will be furious.

ADAM: Just shut up, stop struggling and run.

LUCY: No, I won't shut up. I don't like it out here; I want to get back in the car.

ADAM: No, you don't. Surely you can see what that woman's up to? You don't want to end up being held to ransom in some stinky cellar full of rats and spiders, do you, with nothing to eat but stale bread if you're lucky?

LUCY: You're nuts; Cynthia wouldn't do that. What's got into you?

ADAM: She's hard, that woman, just like my step-mum used to be. I could spot her type a mile off.

LUCY: You don't know anything about her; she's kind. She gave me a coral necklace and she took my aunty out for tea when she got upset at the hospital.

ADAM: Big deal! She was just buttering you up so you'd go off with her and your aunty would never suspect a thing. Anyway, she's blown it. She'll never catch up with us now, not in those daft shoes.

LUCY: You're crazy, you are! I wish I'd never offered to lend you that money, then you'd never have been in the car in the first place.

ADAM: One day you'll realise, it's a good job I was with you today. I probably saved your life. You have to act fast with villains like her. See what happens when you take lifts from people you hardly know? I did warn you, so maybe you'll be more careful in future.

LUCY: Cynthia only wanted to give us a surprise treat. Why do you have to think the worst of everybody? I bet she'd already fixed it up with our folks, and if she had, that's going to make you look pretty silly. Fancy dragging me out of the car like that! You nearly pulled my arm off.

ADAM: Yeah, well, I just saved your skin, so you owe me. Sit yourself down on that rock, ring your uncle on my mobile and get him to come and fetch us. I can't waste any more

time stuck on this moor. I need to
go back and collect that money,
then shoot off to see my dad. It's
getting more urgent by the minute.

LUCY: Well, Mr Clever, it so happens
that I can't ring my uncle now
because he works nights. I don't
know his work number, and even if
I did he wouldn't be able to get
away.

ADAM: Ring your aunt, then. She'll
know what to do.

LUCY: No, she won't. She'll just panic
if she thinks we're out on the moors
on our own, especially now it's
getting dark. Why don't YOU ring
somebody, if that's what you want?

ADAM: All right then, I'll ring my mate
Dave. His dad'll come and fetch us,
but he lives a long way off, so it's
going to take time.

LUCY: Isn't Dave one of your old

school friends from Carfield? Well, you needn't think I'm going all the way over there. I'm off back to Cynthia.

ADAM: Go on then, get kidnapped if you want to, see if I care.

LUCY: (suddenly frightened) Adam, I can't move! My feet are sinking. I'm stuck fast in this squelchy mud. It's a bog! Ring somebody, quick! Anybody! Dial 999.

ADAM: Hang on then – oh, no! My mobile! It's gone; I must have dropped it on the moor somewhere. I know I had it when I jumped out of the car.

LUCY: Well, go and look for it. Hurry up! I can feel myself sinking further.

ADAM: I can't hurry up – I'm stuck as well.

PART 3
MISTAKES ALL ROUND

Vincent Sharkey to Cynthia Blake's mobile, Thursday evening, 14th

– Right then, I've had a good think and here's what you do. Ring the police right away and tell them the kids have run off. You can't think why, you were only taking them for a surprise treat but they must have wanted to tease you, and now you're worried because they haven't come back and you can't see where they are. Act concerned and make sure they know that you're a close friend of the family. Wring your hands and shed a few tears if you can manage it. Best of all, offer to help them search.

– Oh, blow your stilettos! Do it in your stocking feet if you have to.

– *Well, if you drive off and don't say a word they'll be bound to think the worst.*

– *Believe me, they'll track you down later, wherever you hide yourself. Then they'll stick their noses into everything, the cat will be out of the bag and bang goes our master plan.*

Do that to me, girl, and I'll never forgive you.

– *No, you can't come over here and drag me into it. You just stay well away from me until all this dies down. You don't even know me, understand?*

– *Look, Cyn, I'm not going to argue; you just do as I say. You asked for advice, so take it. And just bear this in mind - if those kids happen to get lost and die out on that moor you'll be up for murder. Now get dialling 999.*

Lucy Melling's tape recording, Thursday night, 14th

Mum, you'll never guess what happened today. Talk about excitement! Adam Sykes and me, we both got rescued by police helicopter off Stebbings moor. We're all right, not hurt or anything, so there's no need to worry, but it didn't half cause a stir.

What happened was, that nice Cynthia who's staying at the Wilsons' next door was taking Adam and me out for a surprise treat. We were going to have tea at a cake shop. The trouble was, Adam didn't know her and he got the daft idea that she was trying to kidnap us. As if! He made her stop the car just as we were crossing the moor, then he dragged me out and made me run off with him. Escaping, so he said. Well, then he was going to ring for help on his mobile, only he'd lost it. (He was told not to take that mobile to school any more because it started ringing in the middle of assembly but he hides it inside his shirt and it must have dropped out when we were running.) By then we were stuck in this horrible stinky bog. It was a bit scary, I must admit, and I sank nearly up to my knees, but luckily Cynthia had already rung for help. The police came looking for us right away, because they knew about the bog and it was getting dark.

We could see some cars in the distance, then this helicopter flew over and a man called Mike got lowered down out of it. He grabbed me and we both held on tight to get winched up. I felt a bit dizzy because we were spinning round and round, but Mike kept shouting that we were nearly there. I didn't open my eyes until we got right up to the helicopter, but then I could see for miles, all the lights coming on in Stebbings and the police lights down below. Another man called Steve wrapped me in a blanket and gave me a hot drink out of a flask while Mike went back for Adam.

They took us for a shower at the police station to wash all the mud off us, then they gave us cups of tea and some chocolate and we had to talk to this policewoman. Adam kept going on about being kidnapped but I told her that was just a silly mistake that Adam had made because he panicked. I explained that he'd been having a rough time of it lately so it was no wonder he went off the deep end. Adam got really mad at me for saying that, but the policewoman said not to worry, they would sort it all out and the main thing was that we were both back safe and sound.

I wanted to tell you all this right away in case you'd heard something and were worried. It's sure to be in all the papers. I said I wouldn't go to bed until I'd done this recording, so Aunty M let me stay up to finish it and she'll get it to you first thing tomorrow. Promise me you won't worry, Mum, because honestly there's no need.

I guess I should have been furious with Adam for causing all this mess, but he was really upset and if it had been a real kidnap then I reckon he would have saved my life. He's a pretty quick thinker and he meant well. So we are still friends as far as I'm concerned, which is just as well because Adam is staying with us for the time being.

It turns out his gran collapsed with shock when the police went to tell her what had happened, so she's finished up in hospital. Aunty M said Adam couldn't stay at his gran's house all by himself. She took pity on him and made him a bed up in the spare room. Wasn't that kind of her?

Adam didn't think so, though. He said he didn't want to stop with us, he wanted to go and see his dad, but Aunty M told him that now wasn't a good time. She kept giving Uncle Rob funny looks when she said that, so I reckon there's something going on that I don't know about. He's a bit of a puzzle, that Adam. Nothing for you to worry about, though. You just keep on getting better.

Night night, Mum, and lots of love.

Telephone message from Cynthia Blake to Vincent Sharkey, Thursday night, 14th

I know you're there, Vin Sharkey, whether you pick up or not. So I hope you're listening good when I say I'm disgusted with you and your bright ideas. I'm stuck at Stebbings police station now, as if you hadn't guessed, and I'm likely to be here all night. 'Helping with enquiries', they call it, though I know what name I'd give to it. And I'm only allowed one telephone call, so pin your ears back and listen.

I did what you said – more fool me! – and the cops answered my 999 call all right. In droves! Before you could say 'help' one lot had swooped over in a helicopter because they were worried about the bog. (Never thought of that, did you?) Then the cars started zooming in. There were police all over the place and they were making such a drama out of the whole thing that I panicked, didn't I? It was obvious they were going to find the kids, so I tried to sneak away while they were busy. Didn't get far, though. As soon as they heard the car start up they were after me, and now they've got really suspicious. You wouldn't believe the sort of questions they've been asking me. You'd better get me out of this mess pretty quick. Tell them you knew all about this surprise tea-party. You were supposed to tell the kids' folks, but something important came up and you forgot.

I'm expecting to see you here, Vin Sharkey, and if you don't turn up I

guess I'll have a few interesting little revelations of my own to make to the police.

98

E-mail from Gloria Wilson to Fiona Blake, Friday, 15th

Fee, I tried to ring you earlier but you weren't in. You'll have seen the papers by now though, so you'll know all about the carry-on. Fancy those kids being winched up in a helicopter!

I'm ever so sorry your Cynthia's in trouble with the cops. You must be really upset, but I have to say she's brought it on herself. It was pretty thoughtless and irresponsible, driving off with a couple of kids without telling their folks, surprise treat or not. Rob and Myra were going crazy, as you can imagine. Myra had to fetch Rob home from work, she was in such a state. As for that poor boy's grandmother, apparently she had a funny turn when the police turned up to tell her what had happened. Collapsed on her own doorstep, would you believe? So she's in hospital now, as well, and Rob and Myra have had to take the boy in for the time being, though he keeps shouting that he wants to go home to his dad, ungrateful beggar. All those people upset, just because your Cyn didn't stop to think! Let's hope they realise that's all it was, and let her go before long.

Mind you, I reckon it might take a while. The police are making too much of a meal of it, if you ask me. You'd think they had no real criminals to catch. Two of them, an Inspector and a Sergeant, have even been round here asking all sorts of questions, most of them nothing to do with any of it. We did our best, me and Jim, but they didn't look too happy. They wanted to know why Cynthia had suddenly turned up here after all this time. (Jim had blurted out that we hadn't seen her for fifteen years, trust him!) I said it was the first chance she'd had in a long while to come and see her favourite aunt and uncle, but Jim ruined it all by saying he didn't realise it was against the law to visit your relatives! (I told him off for being sarky to the cops; it doesn't do. But you know what my Jim's like, speak first and think later.)

They wanted to know how well Cynthia knew those kids, and Jim said barely at all, so they asked why take them out to tea, then? They seemed to think it was a funny coincidence that she'd suddenly turned up in Bonnydale at about the same time as the boy. I told them that as far as I knew she'd never even heard of this Adam Sykes before Tuesday, but that she was a private detective, so who knows? They didn't seem to like the idea of that, and I could see the Inspector had made up his mind that your Cyn was up to something. He definitely reckoned it was the boy she was after! He seemed to think she might have been trying to spirit him away before he could be got hold of to

101

give evidence at his step-mum's inquest. Honestly! Makes you wonder, though, doesn't it? Was that the case she was working on? Maybe that boy saw something he shouldn't have; who knows what goes on behind people's closed doors? It's a funny old world, when all's said and done.

The cops asked for your address, so I expect they'll have been over to see you as well by now. What a mess, eh? Still, I expect it can all be sorted out. Let me know how you get on.

Telephone message from Adam Sykes to his friend Dave, Friday, 15th

– *Dave? It's me, Adam. Listen, I've lost my mobile so I'm in a telephone box and my money might run out. I need a big favour, it's really urgent. Can you get your dad to come and pick me up as soon as possible?*

– *I know he's working, but can't he get some time off?*

– *What about after work, then?*

– *All right then, it'll have to be tomorrow morning, but I do wish he could make it today.*

– *You know why; I've got to sort my dad out.*

– *Yeah, I know I said I was coming back to Carfield under my own steam,*

*but I couldn't manage it because of
what happened Thursday night. I
expect you'll have seen it in the papers,
but if not I'll tell you about it later. My
gran's gone to hospital, I think she had
a stroke or something, and I'm stuck
at this daft Lucy Melling's house.*

*   – 'Course I didn't want to stay there
with all this crisis going on, but I
couldn't get the bus because I'm flat
broke. Lucy was going to lend me the
money for the fare, only she went and
told her bossy aunt who put a stop to
it. Now the aunt's made me stay at their
house until everything's sorted out.
She's even taking us to the doctor's this
afternoon for a check-up, would you
believe? She's a right old fusspot.*

*   – Yeah, I did try talking to the police.
There was a policewoman who seemed
a decent sort so I tried her, but she
didn't seem to know what I was on*

about. She just thought I was hysterical
because of getting stuck in this bog.

– I did explain properly. I told her
Dad couldn't have pushed Jenny down
the stairs because I did it, it was an
accident. Jenny pushed ME; she was
always knocking me about, as you
know. So this time I pushed her back,
only a little push, but she slipped on
this mat on the landing and went
skidding down the stairs. She banged
her head on every step; it was awful! I
never meant to kill her and I said so.
But I might as well have saved my
breath; it was all a waste of time. The
policewoman here didn't believe any
of it had ever happened. She just thinks
I'm nuts. Trouble is, I'm not talking to
the right people. I need to get hold of
the ones who are holding my dad.

– Well, listen, you're the only one
who can help me, Dave. If your dad

can't make it today then ask him to
drive over first thing tomorrow
morning and pick me up at my gran's
house, number two, Clifton Road. I'll
make sure I'm over there and I'll wait
for him there for as long as it takes,
but do tell him how urgent it is.

– Great! Thanks, Dave, you're a real
pal; I owe you one.

PART 4
RESOLUTIONS

Adam Sykes at his gran's house, Saturday morning, 16th

Adam was over at 2, Clifton Road by
seven o'clock that Saturday morning,
having sneaked out while the Mellings
were still in bed. He reckoned the car
journey from Carfield to Bonnydale
shouldn't take more than two hours,
even in heavy traffic. He had hoped
Dave's dad would make an early start
and be with him by nine o'clock at the
latest. But two hours passed, then
another hour and another, and still
there was no sign of a car pulling up.
Adam was getting desperate.

Had Dave let him down after all and
refused to pass on the message?
Maybe he didn't want to get mixed up
in it all. Or perhaps his dad had
refused to come, or got lost, or had an
accident on the way? Adam
desperately wanted to ring Dave again

to find out what was going on, but he hadn't any money. Why, oh why, was his gran the only person in the world without a telephone?

Then, when he was just about to explode with anxiety, the doorbell rang.

At last! Adam bounded down the hall and flung open the door. But it wasn't Dave's dad who stood there; it was Lucy Melling.

'What are you doing here?' cried Adam in bitter disappointment.

Lucy explained that her folks were getting anxious because Adam had been away for a long time and had missed his lunch.

'I guessed you'd be here and I promised to fetch you back. I told them you'd be over here collecting some of your things.'

Adam was furious.

'Why can't you leave me alone?' he yelled. 'You've been nothing but trouble. I can't stand people who don't keep their promises. You were supposed to be lending me some money, remember? And if you'd just gone straight home to fetch it I wouldn't be in this mess. None of us would, including my gran.'

'I'm sorry about your gran, but you can't blame me for that. I couldn't lend you the money because my aunty found out and wouldn't let me. She didn't want you to use it to go back home. And you needn't pull that face, it was all for your own good. She said this wasn't the right time for you to be going home, especially since we've got to talk to the police some more.'

'Well you and your precious aunty have ruined everything. It's a matter of life and death, me getting back to my dad, but I can't expect you to understand.'

'Why don't you try me?' invited Lucy gently.

And suddenly that seemed like a good idea. Before he could stop himself, Adam had blurted out the whole story, after which, to his own deep dismay, he burst into tears. His latest arrangement with Dave had obviously fallen through and now he didn't know what to do. He felt utterly forlorn.

'So now you know! I'm a murderer and I'm going to end up in prison.'

''Course you're not! Accidents aren't murder. Even if they were, you're far too young to go to prison, so just calm down.'

Still, Lucy could see that Adam did need to explain things to get his dad off the hook. So far, he hadn't told the police that he had actually pushed his step-mum, just that she had slipped and fallen. So Lucy suggested they'd better find some money after all and get Adam back to Carfield without her aunt finding out.

Adam brightened up, though he knew that was easier said than done.

He told Lucy there was no money anywhere in the house; he'd looked.

'I bet you haven't looked everywhere. Somebody like your gran might hide money all over the place. My gran used to keep money in an old teapot.'

Together they began a search of the house, starting in the kitchen. They looked in every cupboard and every drawer, hopefully exploring anything with a lid. They lifted cushions, felt down the sides of armchairs and sofa, lay flat on the carpet to peer under furniture and even turned the vases over.

Nothing! Not so much as a penny anywhere.

'I told you,' said Adam gloomily.

'Upstairs might be more likely. That OK with you?' Lucy hung back until Adam started up the stairs, then followed.

Adam knew there was no money in his own room so he made straight for his gran's bedroom. Lucy advised him to try all the pockets in the clothes in the wardrobe, and to search through any handbags he found, however old and battered they looked. Adam couldn't even find a handbag. Gran must have only one, which she'd taken to hospital.

In a last desperate effort Adam began searching under the mattress on his gran's bed, sweeping his hands along the dusty bed-springs in the wild hope of encountering a fat wad of notes. Not a chance!

Meantime, Lucy turned to gran's dressing-table. Maybe there was something less obvious there. She remembered vividly the moment when she had discovered the hidden bead in her mother's dressing-table. She pushed and pulled at all the knobs and handles, but to no avail. Miracles obviously didn't happen twice.

She decided to go back home, defy her aunt and sneak out some money without anybody noticing, but as she passed the door of Adam's bedroom she decided to have one last look. The dressing-table there was old, scratched and marked with heat-rings from countless mugs of tea, yet it could still be recognised as good quality furniture. Lucy pulled out the central drawer completely – and noticed a small brass catch behind it.

There was still no money in the secret cavity beyond, just a small, velvet-covered box with a keyhole but no key. Blowing away the dust, Lucy turned the box over and over, wondering how to get it open.

Just then the doorbell rang for a second time and Dave's dad appeared.

'You ready, then?' he called cheerfully to Adam who came charging ecstatically down the stairs.

'Sorry I'm late, but I had to pick your dad up first, then drop him off at the hospital to see your gran. We're going to meet him there as soon as you're ready.'

Adam stood amazed. 'You picked Dad up? You mean, the police have let him go?'

'Sure have! They decided Jenny's fall must have been an accident after all, which is what you told them, and what anybody with any sense knew in the first place. It seems this couple came back yesterday from a holiday abroad, heard about Jenny for the first time and remembered they'd seen your dad that night. He'd been on the way to the pub at the crucial time, and they'd stopped for a chat with him, so that clinched it.'

This was the moment at which Lucy put her hand back into the secret cavity and found the tiny key.

Lucy Melling's tape recording, Sunday, 17th

Mum! Things just get more and more exciting. You'll never guess what's happened now! I found this velvet box in a secret part of Adam's dressing-table and when I opened it I found this massive great diamond. Everybody says it's real, Mum, and it's the biggest and sparkliest you've ever seen, bigger than a bird's egg.

It belongs to Adam's gran, only she didn't know she had it. It was in the dressing-table when she bought it at a second-hand sale. Adam took the diamond to show her in hospital yesterday and she said when she's better she'll sell it and give half the money to Adam's dad. I'm ever so pleased for them, even though I'm sad because Adam's gone home now. I'm going to miss him a lot, but I will see him again. He's promised to come over and bring me a present for finding the diamond, and anyway he'll be visiting his gran quite a lot. He seems to like me a bit better now, so I think we'll always keep in touch.

Tracy sends her love. She's just posted you a card she made herself on the computer. It's a bit cockeyed, but don't laugh, she means well.

Lots of love from everyone in Bonnydale.

Tape recording from Lucy Melling's mum to her daughter, Sunday, 17th

Well, Lucy, here's another surprise, which I hope is as good as your diamond. This is a message coming back to you from your mum who is feeling much, much better.

You seem to have been having a very exciting time while I've been lounging about in hospital, so the doctor thinks I'd better get home soon and calm you down a bit. In the meantime, why don't you come and visit me here? Tape recorders are all very well, but they are nowhere near as good as a face-to-face chat. Come with Aunty Myra tomorrow and bring me some grapes. I could just fancy some – black, with no pips.